Illustrated by Pam Storey
Written by Deborah Campbell-Todd

Published by
Grandreams Limited
435-437 Edgware Road, Little Venice,
London, W2 1TH.

Printed in Hong Kong.

MY FAVOURITE BOOK OF
ANIMAL STORIES

Contents

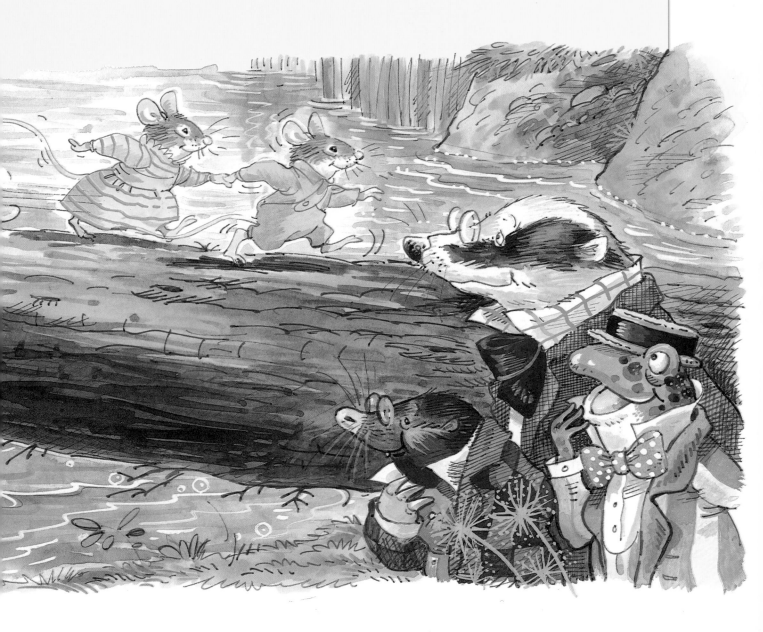

The Race

"The finishing line will be in the middle of the Market Square in Foxtown," announced Badger, the mayor. "You may start as soon as all the car engines are running."

The animals dashed back to their cars, each determined to be first away.

It was the day of the annual Vintage Car Race. Most of the animals were taking part.

Fox had a beautiful red car with glossy leather seats.

Mole's car was dark green. Mrs Mole jumped into the car, holding onto her large hat. Mole stood by to crank the car to start it.

10

Rabbit bounced into a bright blue car and tooted his horn, eager to be off.

Owl pulled his goggles down over his eyes, and sat on his motorcycle.

"Ready, steady," began Mayor Badger.

Some of the engines roared into life, others just spluttered and put-putted into a smoky start.

"Go!" shouted Mayor Badger, dropping the flag.

"Hurray!" shouted the animals, as they started off down the lane. Horns tooted and bells rang as the old cars disappeared in a cloud of smoke.

Mayor Badger went to the station to catch the train to

Foxtown to be waiting at the finishing line.

Fox was in the lead, his bright red car pulling away from the others.

"I'll win! I'll win!" he shouted.

"Oh, no, you won't," said Owl on his motorcycle as he pulled alongside.

"Watch out for me!" yelled Mole, as he and Mrs Mole dashed by the other two animals as they argued. The Moles took the lead, but Mole wasn't looking as he overtook.

"Mr Mole!" shouted Mrs Mole, as he left the road and drove into a stream. The little green car went put! put! and then stopped. It wouldn't start again.

"Now we'll have to walk," said Mrs Mole. "If only you had been looking where you were going and not where you had been!"

"We'll catch the train from the village," said Mole, and the two set off for the station to wait for the next train to Foxtown.

The other cars went dashing past the Moles' green car.

Rabbit raced into the lead,

and pulled far ahead. In the distance he saw a cart being pulled by a horse. He dashed past it, shouting, "Buy a car! It's a lot quicker than that old thing!"

"That may be," said Squirrel, the driver. "But speed isn't everything."

Rabbit raced on and was getting closer to Foxtown.

"Only the hill to go!" he chuckled.

But then Rabbit had to go along a very stony road. The silly Rabbit didn't slow down.

Pop! Pop! Two of his tyres burst!

"Oh no," sobbed Rabbit. "One tyre I can change, but not two!"

He watched as the other cars came up to him. They saw his flat tyres and slowed down and went safely down the road.

Ten minutes later, the horse and cart came into view.

"Can I help?" asked Squirrel.

"I'm sorry I was so rude," said Rabbit.

"Let's hitch up the horse to the car, and we'll tow you to the finishing line," said Squirrel.

13

The other cars had reached the steep hill that led into Foxtown. All they had to do was get to the top!

There was much muttering as the cars went slower and slower as they climbed the hill.

"Come on," Fox said to his little red car which was going very slowly. "You can't let me down. I know you can do it."

But his little red car reached the top of the hill, sputtered and stopped, steam pouring from the engine.

"Oh, little car," sighed Fox, and he watched the other cars as they went past.

"Come on, Fox. On you get!" yelled Owl from his motorcycle. "We'll get there yet!"

Fox jumped up behind Owl and the two set off again, down the hill.

The finishing line was in sight, and Mayor Badger was waiting with the flag.

Vroom! Vroom! Beep! Beep! Toot! went the cars as they rushed down to the market square.

Who was going to win?

The cars were neck and neck! The flag went down!

The winner was ..... Mouse - by a whisker!

Mole and Mrs Mole arrived on the next train.

Owl, with Fox behind him came second, and Rabbit had a very interesting talk with Squirrel about horses, and came in last!

The Three Bears' Day Out

"Oh, great! A day at Nana and Grandad's!" shouted Bod.

"Shh!" said his big sister Posie. "I want to check my bag again."

"We're only going for the day!" said Bod. "Why do you need a bag?"

"I want to take my book about the princess," said Posie.

"Come along, all of you!" called Daddy Bear. "Time to go!" He picked up Baby Em and off they went.

Nana and Grandad Bear lived in the next village, so the three little bears were soon there.

"Grandad and I have been busy," said Nana. "Come with us."

Nana led Posie to her sewing room, and Grandad led Bod to his shed. Bod became very

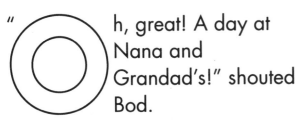

excited when he saw where they were going. It could mean just one thing - Grandad had made something.

"What is it Grandad?" asked Bod. "What's it going to be?"

"Just wait, little Bear," laughed Grandad.

Nana and Posie were in the sewing room where Nana had something to show Posie.

"A little bird tells me you like fairy tales about princesses," Nana said to Posie.

Posie nodded, and Nana took something from the table and held it up to Posie.

"A good fit, I think," said Nana, and she slipped a dress over Posie's head. But it was no ordinary dress. It was just like the dress the princess wore in her favourite story!

"Nana!" cried Posie, and she

gave her Nana a great big hug. "It's just what I always wanted! Thank you, Nana." She did a twirl.

"Lovely!" said Nana.

"Can I show Bod?" asked Posie.

"Off you go, but be careful!" said Nana and she smiled as Posie ran out.

"Bod! Bod! Look at me!" cried Posie as she ran down the garden.

Bod was in the shed with his Grandad.

"Wow! Grandad - is that for me?" asked Bod.

"It's for both of us," said Grandad, holding up the beautiful red and white kite he had made. "The next time it's windy, I'll take you up onto the hill and we'll fly it together."

"Oh, that's wonderful, Grandad, thank you!" And Bod gave his Grandad a great big hug.

"And I've made this for Baby Em," added Grandad, and he pointed to a chair in the corner. It was just like the ordinary chairs in the kitchen, but on much longer legs!

"Baby Em can eat with us now!" said Bod.

Posie came in through the door. "Look! Look! I'm just like a princess. The princess in my book! Nana made it for me!"

"Grandad has made me a kite, and we're going to fly it next time it's windy!" cried Bod. "And look what he has made for Baby Em."

The two little bears then left to tell Baby Em about her new high-chair.

Later that day when the little bears were at home, and their Daddy had read them a story, Bod said, "Can we take a present to Nana and Grandad to say thank you?"

"What do you think he would like?" asked Daddy.

"Grandad loves honey with his toast in the morning, and so does Nana," said Posie. "We'll use our pocket money to buy a jar of honey."

And the next morning, Posie and Bod went to the village shop and bought a jar of honey.

Nana and Grandad were very happy with their present, and have toast and honey every morning, especially when the three little bears come to visit.

Helpful Toby

"Fox, have you seen my tea-towels?" asked Mrs Fox, as she took the laundry in. There were a few gaps on the washing line. "And where's the other basket?"

"Basket, what basket?" asked Fox as he rummaged in his shed.

Down the lane, Owl looked out from his tree house.

"Hello-o!" came a voice,

"Can I come up?"

"Yes, Mouse, use the ladder as usual," said Owl.

"The ladder's not there," said Mouse.

"Not there?" said Owl, and he flew down to the ground. He kept a ladder up to his house so that those animals who could not fly could still get up to see him.

Mouse waited at the bottom.

"Look," he pointed. "No ladder."

And indeed, there was no ladder.

"Well, I say," said Owl, and he scratched the top of his head.

"Owl! Mouse!" It was Mole.

"Good morning Mole," said Owl.

"Hello," said Mole. "Something strange is happening. Things have gone missing in the village. I've just seen Mr and Mrs Fox. There are some tea-towels and a basket missing. Rabbit's rocking chair has disappeared from his veranda, and my bell has gone. Some hot fruit pies disappeared from Badger's table and..."

"Owl's ladder has gone," added Mouse. "And so has my porch lantern!"

"How strange," said Owl. "Ah, here are Fox and Badger. Maybe they know something." Fox and Badger walked up to them.

"It's very odd," said Fox. "They're such strange things to go missing. They're not worth anything. Who could want our tea-towels or laundry basket?"

"Or my wife's fruit pies?" said Badger. "What do you make of it, Owl?"

"Your ladder too!" exclaimed Fox, as he looked at Owl's tree.

The friends stood a moment.

"We need to leave some bait," said Fox.

"Good idea," declared Owl.

"My wheelbarrow!" said Mole. "Whoever it is will need something to take the things away!"

"Let's leave it behind Mole's house, and I'll watch from my tree," said Owl. "I'll yell if I see anyone."

The wheelbarrow was put where Owl could see it.

It was a warm sunny day, and Owl began to doze in the heat.

"I really am better at night," he muttered as he shook himself to keep awake. "Hello, what's that?"

A small figure was walking into Mole's garden. It was wearing a great big hat and a long coat.

"I think it's a bit too hot for that lot," said Owl. "And that is

Mrs Mouse's hat, and that is definitely not Mrs Mouse!"

Owl swooped down from his tree, and called out, "You-hoo, stop there!"

The figure jumped with fright, and as Owl landed, it disappeared.

"Where has he gone?" asked Owl.

"Who is it?" asked Fox, as he ran into the garden.

"Have you got him?" said Mole.

They looked around. "There's no one here," said Badger.

"There was!" said Owl, looking around. "And there's his hat."

"That's Mrs Mouse's hat!" squeaked Mouse.

"And Mrs Badger's gardening coat," said Badger.

There was a struggle beneath the wheelbarrow.

"Got you!" said Fox, and he appeared holding a small rabbit.

"Let me go!" cried the little rabbit.

"Where's your mother?" asked Owl.

"In an old burrow by the big

oak tree," said the little rabbit.

The animals walked with the rabbit out of the village to the oak tree.

Mrs Rabbit came running to meet them.

"Toby!" she cried. "Where have you been? Has he been naughty?"

Badger was holding little Toby.

"Well..." began Fox.

"Are you living here?" asked Mole.

"Yes," nodded Mrs Rabbit. "My old home was flooded and we had to move very quickly, I had to leave everything behind."

"I was just trying to help," said Toby. "The baby needed a bed and cover."

"The basket and tea-towels?" asked Fox, Toby nodded.

"Mum needs a chair to sit in, and some way to tell us it's dinnertime," said Toby.

"The rocking chair and bell," said Mole.

"It was dark in the burrow."

"The lantern," said Mouse.

"Wood for the fire?" said Toby, looking up at Owl.

"My ladder?" asked Owl.

"And something for dinnertime," said Badger. "The fruit pies, perhaps?"

Toby nodded. "I'm sorry," he said. "I shouldn't have taken them."

"Well, let's see if we can help you and your family. Come to me tomorrow, Toby, and I'll show you how to make some stools and a table," said Badger.

"Mrs Mole will take you to the shop, Mrs Rabbit," said Mole. "Everyone in the village will help

when they hear what has happened."

"Welcome to the village," said Mouse. "Keep the lantern, and the bits and pieces. I'm sure we'll be able to manage."

"We'll go back and tell everyone that we have new neighbours," said Fox.

The animals turned to go, leaving Toby with his mother.

"Badger, while you are making the stools, do you think you can make a ladder for me?" Owl asked Badger. "I'm sure little Toby will be able to help." He looked back at little Toby and winked.

The Croaks And The Oinks

"Croak! Croak! Ribbet! Croak! Croak! Croak! Ribbet! Croak! Ribbet!

"Perfect!" croaked Gilbert, the choir's conductor. "If you sing like that for the the Chamberlain, the 'Croaks' will be asked to perform at every party up to Christmas!"

"But what about Baron Nogood and his choir?" asked a small frog.

"Don't worry about him," said Gilbert. "Once the Chamberlain hears us, the 'Oinks' will have to take their trotters and leave the stage to us!"

Meanwhile, in the main sty, Baron Nogood was rehearsing his chorus, the 'Oinks', and things were not going well.

"Read the music!" he cried. "Some of you are grunting where you should be squeaking. This should sound musical! Again, from the top!"

The 'Oinks' began their piece again.

Baron Nogood waved his baton around, and as it was not in time to the music, various pigs started at different times and the result was a dreadful mixture of grunting, squealing and oinking.

"Stop! Stop!" cried the Baron. At that moment a young piglet ran up.

"I've just been listening to the 'Croaks'," he said.

"And?" asked Baron Nogood.

"They're ready," said the piglet. "And they're very good."

"Good!" exclaimed the Baron. "They haven't heard the

'Oinks' yet!"

"But Baron," said Percy, who sang bass. "We're nowhere near ready!"

"No matter," declared Baron Nogood. "That will come." He turned to the piglet. "Where are they? Show me."

The piglet led the Baron to the millpond, and as they drew closer the sound of the 'Croaks' singing drifted across the water.

"Isn't that lovely?" said the piglet dreamily, as he stopped to listen.

"Sounds like a lot of croaking to me," said Baron Nogood. "Nothing tuneful!" He turned back, already plotting and scheming.

"There must be some way," he muttered.

The piglet sneezed softly behind him.

"You can't sing with a cold, you know," said the Baron, and that set him thinking.

A week later, the Chamberlain came to hear the two choirs, to decide who would sing at the ball.

The 'Oinks' had been practising hard, and were now singing together and in time, much to Baron Nogood's delight. "Hear my little pigs sing," the Baron said to the Chamberlain and Gilbert. "You won't need another choir for the masked ball." The frogs stood in their places, their songbooks on the stands in front of them. Gilbert tapped his music stand and the frogs opened their books. Powder flew out of the pages, into the frogs' faces. And they began to sneeze! They sneezed and sneezed, jumping around with every sneeze! Their eyes were

streaming and there were not
enough handkerchiefs to go
around.

Gilbert was furious. "You did
that!" he said to Baron Nogood.

"What did I do?" asked the
Baron innocently.

"Sneezing - Aa-aa-choo! -
powder!" sneezed Gilbert.

"You can't possibly sing,"
said the Chamberlain. "I'll hear
the 'Oinks' now." Baron Nogood
stood in front of the 'Oinks' and
they sang their song.

The Chamberlain had no
choice. He had to choose the
'Oinks' to perform at the masked
ball.

The evening of the masked
ball at last arrived. It had been
raining all week and this did not
suit the 'Oinks'. They all seemed
to be going down with colds in
the damp weather.

"By dose is blocked," said
Percy.

"My throat is sore," said
another pig, huskily.

Even Baron Nogood was poorly.

"You can't sing like that!" said the Chamberlain. "I'm going to see Gilbert."

The Chamberlain ran down the millpond and called for Gilbert.

"We need you," he told Gilbert. "The 'Oinks' are ill. Can the 'Croaks' perform?"

"We'll be there in ten minutes," said Gilbert. He rounded up the 'Croaks' and they ran up to the house.

"No!" said Baron Nogood, when he saw the 'Croaks'. "The 'Oinks' should be singing."

"But Baron, we feel really ill," said Percy. The 'Oinks' began coughing and sneezing.

"This is hopeless," said the Baron, and he stomped out of the house. As he walked down the drive in the pouring rain, he heard the music start.

"Aaa-choo!" he sneezed. At the sty, he settled down to sleep.

At the ball, the 'Croaks' were singing, and one by one the pigs put away their handkerchiefs. The dancers were in full swing.

All the guests were enjoying themselves.

As the Baron drifted off to sleep, the 'Croaks' began singing again.

'Croak! Croak! Ribbet! Croak! Croak! Croak! Oink! Croak! Ribbet!"

'Was that one of my 'Oinks'?' thought the Baron sleepily.

The 'Oinks' had all put away their handkerchiefs, and were standing with the 'Croaks'.

"We didn't like the way Baron Nogood cheated at the rehearsal," Percy told Gilbert.

"He used sneezing powder in your hankies. We did the same and it did the trick! Sneezes galore!"
asked Gilbert.

"His cold is real!" laughed Percy.

For the next song, the 'Croaks' and 'Oinks' joined forces and were the hit of the ball.

From then on the 'Croaks' and 'Oinks' sang together, and at every party up to Christmas.

Poor Baron Nogood was out of sorts until Easter!

Owl's New Home

Mrs Mole met Mrs Fox outside the village shop on a rather windy morning.

"A little blowy," said Mrs Fox, as she held onto her hat.

"Mrs Frog says it will get stronger," said Mrs Mole. "She told me her husband can feel it in his bones."

"Well, if he says that I'd best be off," said Mrs Fox and Mrs Mole watched in amazement as an umbrella went flying down the lane, with Mrs Mouse chasing along behind.

Mayor Badger had just turned the corner and caught the runaway umbrella squarely on the knees.

"Oh, thank you, Mayor," squeaked Mrs Mouse, as she caught up with her umbrella. "I don't know where it would have stopped if you hadn't caught it!" He rubbed his sore knee, and handed the umbrella safely down to Mrs Mouse. "I wouldn't put it up again," he said.

"Never fear, I'm off home now," said Mrs Mouse. "The next gust, it will be me bowling down the road."

Mrs Mouse scurried off home, pausing just to wave to Mrs Mole. "Time to go!" said Mrs

Fox, and she and Mrs Mole each headed for home.

By mid-afternoon the wind had picked up.

Mrs Fox put anything that could be blown away in Fox's shed.

Mrs Mole took in her laundry before it sailed away.

Mrs Mouse stayed indoors - she definitely did not want to be blown away! By sunset, trees were swaying in the wind. Twigs and small branches were breaking off.

"A night to stay by a roaring fire," said Fox, as he rubbed his hands in front of the grate. "Frog's bones are never wrong."

"Do you suppose Owl will be all right in his house?" asked Mrs Fox. "We've not had a storm quite as strong as this for some

time."

"Old Owl?" said Fox. "He'll be fine. Remember the storm of '87? His tree stood up to that. He'll probably not even wake up!"

Later that night an almighty crash sounded through the village. Some of the animals who were awake wondered which tree had come crashing down.

Fox did not even wake up.

When dawn broke, the animals crept out of their houses to see the damage.

"Goodness!" said Mayor Badger.

Branches were strewn everywhere along the lane, tiles were missing from roofs, and the village shop sign was in the stream! The swing on Mrs Mole's veranda was upside down in the garden. The gnomes in Mrs Fox's garden were in her pond!

Mrs Mouse's chimney was in pieces on the path.

But worst of all was poor Owl's house.

His lovely tree house was

34

now in pieces as his tree lay where it had crashed across the green.

Poor Owl sat on a post, surveying the wreckage of his home. He was cold and wet, his feathers bedraggled and soaked. "You come with me," said Mrs Fox. "We'll put those wet feet in a hot mustard bath. Half an hour by the fire and a hot cup of tea will work wonders."

She led Owl back to her house.

"I never thought it would come down," sighed Owl. "I thought it could stand through anything."

Fox met them at the door. "Any trees down, then?" he asked, with a smile.

"Yes, mine," sighed Owl.

"Your tree!" exclaimed Fox. "But it stood through '87's storm. Why not this one?"

"It must have been weakened," said Owl. "It's lying across the green now, and crosses the stream at the bottom."

Owl was bustled indoors by Mrs Fox, and was soon steaming

in front of the fire. Fox hurried to the village green.

He met Badger, Mole and Frog by the ruins of Owl's house. There was not a lot to be saved. Cups, saucers and plates were broken, but there was a picture of Owl's parents that could be reframed.

"I never thought this would happen," said Mole.

"I thought it was here to stay after '87," said Frog, shaking his head.

"Still," said Badger. "It shouldn't go to waste. Have you seen where it has landed? Right where we decided the new bridge should go!" Some of the smaller animals were already scurrying over the fallen tree where it lay across the stream.

"Makes a great bridge," said Mouse as he came up to them. "I've checked on Mrs Rabbit, Toby and the little ones. A few branches off the old oak but it's OK. Not like Owl's tree."

Toby followed along.

"What will Mr Owl do for a

home now?" he asked.

"He can stay with us until he finds somewhere else," said Fox.

"He needs a new home, doesn't he?" said Toby.

"If we cut the tree off here, and over there," said Badger. "What, Toby - yes, a new home, soon. Trim away some branches. Rope between the rest and it will be a very useful bridge. A little work later on it and it can be permanent."

The animals stood talking, considering the fallen tree as the new bridge.

Toby wandered off. Owl needed a new home and he was determined to find it.

He already had an idea. The other animals would be busy with the bridge, so he went to Squirrel.

"I need someone who can climb," he explained to Squirrel.

Squirrel's home was perfectly safe, and so he left Mrs Squirrel sharing out some nuts for breakfast and went with young Toby.

"It's a place I saw when I was exploring," said Toby.

Toby led Squirrel to an old barn hidden in the woods not far from the village.

"It's perfect here for Owl," said Toby. "But I can't see in the attic."

Squirrel scrambled up into the attic. He pulled old haybales around and looked in the corners.

"Aaa-choo!" he sneezed. "There are plenty of places up here," he called to Toby. "And there's a little window up on this side, so he can have plenty of light. I'll get Mrs Squirrel to take a look. Well done, Toby it's perfect!"

Some time later Mrs Squirrel, with some help from her cousins, took charge of the cleaning of the attic.

Much sneezing and coughing and billowing dust showed the work to be done.

"This hasn't been used for years," called Mrs Squirrel. "And look here!"

She took an old blanket away that was covering something in the shadows. It was an old rocking chair!

"Owl will love that!"

exclaimed Toby.

The Rabbits and the Squirrels worked on the barn all week, while the other animals continued their work in the village.

"I need to get a message to my cousin in Woodville," said Mole. "Where is Toby? I've hardly seen him."

"I wanted to show him how we were going to cut this," said Badger. "But he's just not been here to see any of it."

Exactly a week after the storm the bridge was ready.

"We'll have a grand opening, and Owl can cut the ribbon," said Badger. "After all, it was his tree."

The animals gathered on the green, and Owl cut the ribbon.

"It was my home," he said, "but at least it's been useful. May I declare this bridge officially open!"

He cut the ribbon and the animals started to cross back and forth.

Fox gave Owl the picture of his parents which had been reframed.

"All I need now is a new home to put it in," sighed Owl.

"Toby can help with that," said Squirrel. "Come with us."

Owl followed, and so did the other animals, puzzled by

Squirrel's comment.

Squirrel led the way to the clearing in the wood - and there stood the barn. But now it was clean and tidy. The window was sparkling and sunlight shone into the attic. The rocking chair, with a brand new cushion on it, stood on a rug in the centre.

"For me!" exclaimed Owl. Toby nodded.

Owl flew up, clutching his parent's picture.

He walked around his new home.

"And we wondered what you were doing," said Badger. "This is a very thoughtful and kind thing to do for Owl."

"You said he needed a new home, and I knew this barn was here, and hadn't been used. I couldn't have done it without Squirrel," said Toby.

Meanwhile Owl was sitting in his new chair, rocking gently. He smiled down at Toby. He now had somewhere to put his picture.

A White Christmas

" It's the last day of school, Toby," said Mrs Rabbit, wrapping a scarf around the young rabbit's neck. "Next week it will be Christmas!"

"I hope it snows before then," said Toby. "I'd love a white Christmas."

"There's the village Christmas Eve snow party," said Mrs Rabbit. "So it has to snow for Christmas Eve!"

Toby went off to school, joining his little friends for the last day before Christmas.

All the animals were busy for

the next week, preparing for the Christmas Eve party and Christmas Day itself.

The days passed, but there was no sign of snow.

Owl went to see Fox and Mole.

"We'll have to do something about the party," said Fox. "We can't have a snow party without snow!"

"I've had an idea," said Owl. "I've had a word with the geese and the ducks who live in the house by the pond. They're all in agreement."

"Agreement to what?" asked Mole.

"We'll hold the party in my barn," said Owl. "It's the biggest house in the village. Everyone can get in there. And there's more room for us birds to do our stuff!"

"What stuff?" asked Fox, as puzzled as Mole.

"Feathers!" said Owl. "We've all been collecting our feathers for pillows and quilts, so we'll use them as snow!"

"What a brilliant idea!" said Fox and Mole together.

"Do you think so?" asked Owl, puffing himself up. "I rather thought so too."

"You'll fly around, dropping them over us at the end of the party!" said Mole. "Just like snow!" said Fox.

"And then we collect the feathers and use them for pillows and quilts, as we were going to do," said Owl. "But not a word to anyone. It has to be a surprise."

On Christmas Eve, a dry and

sunny day, the animals took their party food to Owl's barn.

Mrs Fox organised the tables. Mrs Mole and Mrs Mouse found enough paper cups and plates for everyone to use. The squirrels scurried around decorating the barn.

"I have some dandelion wine," said Mrs Rabbit.

"There's blackcurrant jelly," said Mrs Mouse. "And raspberry cups. All those blackberries in the autumn made some lovely jam."

"I've baked dozens of rolls," said Mrs Badger. "And buns and scones."

"Cream from the farm," said Mrs Fox.

"A feast!" said Fox, leaning over the table, about to take a raspberry cup. Mrs Fox tapped his fingers.

"Just a taste, my dear," said Fox, smiling.

"You'll just have to wait," said Mrs Fox.

Evening drew in, and lamps were lit outside all the houses. Trees had Christmas lights on them.

The animals started arriving at Owl's barn. The whole barn was decorated from floor to roof

with holly, ivy and mistletoe. Red ribbons went from beam to beam. Lamps were hanging on the walls and the whole place looked very festive. An enormous Christmas tree stood at the end of the barn.

All the animals were dressed in their party best. When they were all there, they gathered around the tree and sang carols.

Badger disappeared briefly to reappear dressed as Santa Claus.

"Santa asked me to deliver these," said Badger, in his gruff voice to the young animals gathered around him. They soon worked out who was behind the beard.

They unwrapped their presents, showing their parents what Santa Claus had sent.

"Time to eat!" called Mrs Badger, taking the covers from the tables.

And what a feast the animals had! Rolls and buns, scones and jellies! Everything was eaten - not a crumb was left!

"Friends!" Owl called to the animals from his attic. "As you know, this is the animal Christmas Eve snow party. But we've had no snow. So we have come up with our own way of making this a snow party."

He flew out over the animals.

"It's snowtime!" he called, and all the geese and ducks took to their wings, carrying sacks up to the attic. And they opened the sacks and started scattering out handfuls of feathers!

The feathers flew out over the animals, falling gently.

"They look just like snow!" cried Toby.

"Oh, how clever!" cried Mrs Fox.

"This makes it really Christmassy now," said Mrs Mouse, as a small feather landed on her nose. "Aatishoo!" she sneezed.

The animals grabbed handfuls of feathers and threw them up in the air.

"It's not as cold, or as wet as snow!" said Mrs Rabbit.

"And Owl can put them in pillows and quilts when we're finished," said Fox.

"So Owl saved the day and the party!" said Badger. "Three cheers for Owl!"

The animals all hip-hoorayed and Owl stood there with a smile.

Squirrel then came up to the other animals.

"Has anyone looked outside recently?" he asked.

The animals were puzzled and then Fox dashed to the barn door and peeped outside.

Then he threw both doors open.

"Ooh!" sighed the animals. "Look!"

It was snowing gently. It had been snowing for a while, as the ground was covered. The trees wore a light covering of snow.

"It must have started when the party began," said Fox. "And we were having so much fun, we didn't notice!"

"Well, it's a lovely end to the Christmas Eve party," said Badger.

The animals agreed and before long, they were setting out for home.

Off they went, calling out to each other, "Happy Christmas!"

"Happy Christmas Owl," Fox and Mole called, as they left. "We'll look forward to the new pillows and quilts!"

"Happy Christmas!" called Owl.

All The Fun Of The Fair

Bod woke up early one Saturday morning. The fair was coming to he village! He jumped out of bed, and ran to his sister Posie's room.

"Quick, Posie, get out of bed," he said, as he pulled back her cover. "The fair arrives today. Let's look at the green."

Posie jumped up and followed her brother to the windows at the front of their house.

"Look!" cried Bod.

Posie jumped up beside him and looked to see the bright caravans and trailers already on the green.

"They arrived in the night, while you were asleep," their Daddy called up the stairs to them. "Come and have some breakfast. We'll go to the fair when it's all set up, after lunch."

The two small bears ran downstairs to their breakfast. Baby Em was already in her high chair eating hers. She laughed at her big brother and sister to welcome them and clapped her hands.

48

Breakfast was eaten very quickly and the two bears were soon washed and dressed. The morning seemed to drag by. Baby Em had her usual nap. Bod tried to read a book. Posie spent some time in the treehouse. But every so often the bears would go back to the window to see the fair taking shape.

Just after breakfast, the carousel was up. A bit before their snack the helter-skelter was completed. When Baby Em woke up, the coconut shy was ready. And then it was lunch time.

And then the bears were off to the fair. Posie and Bod skipped down the path leading to the green.

Then they saw all the tents and sideshows. There were flags and bunting hanging from tent to tent. There were stripy tents and red tents and blue tents. There was the coconut shy, a haunted house, the carousel and the helter-skelter, giant swing boats and a big hot air balloon giving rides.

"Ooh!" declared Posie and Bod. "What first?"
The two bears went from ride to ride and had a go on everything! They even had some candy floss!

On the far side of the fair was a red-striped tent with a great big sign outside "Madame Min - fortune teller".

There was quite a queue to see her and as somebody went in, Bod looked in the tent. He saw a woman sitting at a table with a glass ball in front of her. She wore a spotted scarf and great golden earrings.

"Come in," he heard her say and the visitor sat on a chair in front of her, and then the tent door closed.

"What is she doing?" Bod asked his father.

"She tells you your fortune," said Daddy Bear. "She gazes into her crystal ball and tells you what she sees."

"Really?" said Bod. "Look, there's Posie. What has she won?"

Posie was proudly carrying a coconut she had won at the shy.

"Time to go now," said Daddy Bear.

The Bears returned home in time for tea. After tea, Bod disappeared. "I just have to do

50

something," he said as he ran
out of the room.

  Half an hour later, Bod called
out from his bedroom.

"Fortunes read!" he called. "Come and have your fortune read!" Mummy and Daddy Bear looked at each other.

"What is he up to now?" asked Mummy.

The Bears went upstairs and Posie pushed open Bod's bedroom door.

Bod was sitting at his little table with something in front of him.

Posie looked closer.

"Let me gaze into my crystal ball," said Bod, "and I will tell you your future."

Bod's crystal ball was one of his Mummy's bowls with her twinkly scarf stuffed into it. On his head he had tied one of her dusters.

"What's that hanging from your ears?" asked Posie, looking even closer.

"Curtain rings," said Bod. "Now, I'm Wizard Wonder - I'm here to tell you your future."

Posie sat own. "Go on then," she said.

Bod waved his hands over the

twinkly scarf. "Your name is Posie," he said.

"I know that," said Posie.

"Nana and Grandpa will be here for the day tomorrow!" declared Bod.

"They're away, Bod," said his Mummy. "You know that."

"My crystal ball tells me they will be here," said Bod.

"I'd better go and make a cake, then," said Mummy. "And can I have my duster back when you've finished."

"Oh, Mum!" said Bod. "It's a magic scarf!"

"Speaking of scarves...." said Mummy, and she went to make a cake.

"Nana and Grandpa will be here tomorrow," said Bod. "I wished them here!"

"Anything else?" asked Posie.

"It will be....a chocolate cake!" he said, sniffing the air.

Daddy laughed. "You can smell that! Come on. Time for bed for you two now."

The three little bears were soon asleep after their busy day.

Sunday morning dawned and Bod was up early.

"I'm waiting for Nana and Grandpa," he told his Mummy and Daddy.

Later, after breakfast there was a knock at the door. Who could it be?

"Nana!" cried Posie.

"Grandpa!" cried Bod.

Little Em clapped her hands.

Mummy and Daddy Bear were amazed!

"The weather was bad so we came home early," said Nana. "We thought we'd come and say 'hello'."

"I told you," said Bod. "Wizard Wonder is never wrong!"

"Wizard Wonder?" asked Nana.

"It's a long story," said Mummy.

"Anyone want to go to the fair this afternoon?" asked Grandpa. "Is Madame Min there this year?"

Mummy and Daddy Bear groaned, while Posie and Bod burst out laughing.

Captain Angelo And The Treasure

"**P**repare to set sail!" called Captain Angelo. "Right, Cap'n!" said Dandy, the first mate.

It was a bright sunny day and the Yankee Doodle puffed up her sails in the breeze, and the little round ship was off.

Captain Angelo hadn't actually been a captain for very long. He had wandered into the little port of Seavale, considering his future, when he found himself helping someone who had fallen from his horse. The rider was an old sea dog.

"Can't sail me boat any more!" declared the old sailor, as Angelo helped him to his house. "Here, you can have it."

"Me!" declared Angelo in surprise. "But I've never sailed a boat before."

"Time to learn, then," said the old dog. "And it's time for me to retire!

"But, I'm also a cat!" said Angelo.

The old dog peered closer. "So you are. You'll be better on your feet, then! Two conditions, though. One, you keep my young brother on as first mate, and two,

the parrot stays with the boat. You don't send him to me. The boat's in the harbour. She's called Yankee Doodle. Brother's called Dandy."

"And the parrot?" asked Angelo.

"Sorry," said the old dog.

"The parrot?" repeated Angelo.

"Sorry - that's its name." It wasn't far to the harbour, and Angelo soon found the Yankee Doodle.

He went up the gangplank and found Dandy sorting some ropes. He looked just like his older brother. Angelo explained what had happened, and Dandy went to see his brother.

He soon returned. "Where

are we off to then, Cap'n?" he asked Angelo.

"You don't mind?" asked Angelo.

"I like being first mate," declared Dandy. "I don't want to be cap'n, Cap'n.

"Is there anywhere you'd like to go?" asked Angelo.

"Well, there is," said Dandy. "Hold on a moment."

Dandy scurried below deck and returned moments later with an old book. "We could try and find this," suggested Dandy. "It's

a treasure map. My brother always pooh-poohed it, so we never looked. But there might be something in it.

"Treasure!" declared Angelo. "Why not? Where do we start?

"Sorry!" came a sudden squawk, and a flash of green feathers flew past to land on the deck rail.

"This is Sorry?" asked Angelo.

"Correct," said Dandy. "Just ignore him. Maybe he'll go and stay with my brother."

"I'm afraid not," said Angelo. "That was the second condition. Sorry stays with the Yankee Doodle.

"Well, maybe we can lose him in a tropical storm!" suggested Dandy.

"You don't get on?" asked Angelo.

"Just wait," said Dandy.

Angelo soon learned what Dandy meant. The parrot's entire vocabulary was made up of just one word - sorry. By the end of the first day, when Angelo was learning about the ship from Dandy, he understood why Dandy's brother didn't want the parrot back!

A few days later, the Yankee Doodle was off, exploring the coast nearby, while Captain Angelo learned about the shop.

And now it was their first voyage together.

"Head due north," declared Captain Angelo. "That's what the map says."

Angelo and Dandy had spent the previous evening studying the map, trying to make head or tail of the clues. They now had a rough idea of where to go.

They had to go north to find a 'camel's back', and then east for the 'crossed tails'. South east would take them to the 'dragon's breath' and then west to 'finger rock'.

The little boat headed north, and after a few days, Angelo began to wonder if they had been right. The following morning it was misty and the little ship travelled slowly.

Dandy was in the crow's nest keeping a look-out.

"Mist breaking ahead!" he called, and he scurried down to the deck.

The mist parted and there in front was an island.

"Look!" cried Angelo. "There are two hills! It looks just like a camel's back! We're on our way!"

"Then we head east," said Dandy. "Towards the 'crossed tails', whatever they may be."

The little ship changed direction and headed east, towards the morning sun.

Two days later, they came across a second island.

"Crossed tails," said Dandy. "Where are 'crossed tails'?"

"Sorry!" squawked Sorry, as it flew up suddenly.

Angelo looked up at the parrot and saw the high cliff behind the trees. "The waterfalls!" he cried. "Look! They fall down the cliff like tails, and

they cross! Thank you, Sorry!"

"South east for the 'dragon's breath', then," said Dandy.

This trip took a little longer and it was several days before they saw land again. One afternoon, they saw a great cloud of smoke rising in the sky.

Dandy and Angelo looked at each other.

As they drew closer to the

island they realised that it was a smoking volcano! "'Dragon's breath'!" said Dandy. "Quick, west for the 'finger rock!'"

The little ship shot off westwards, leaving the smoking island behind them. "I'm glad we didn't have to land there!" said Angelo.

A few days later, the Yankee Doodle reached a small island.

But there was no 'finger rock' to be seen!

Dandy rowed them to shore.

On the beach, there was still no sign of 'finger rock'.

Sorry shot off down a path between the trees.

"We'll have to follow him," said Angelo. The parrot had disappeared, but they could hear him squawking ahead.

"He can see more from in the air," said Dandy.

The two followed the parrot's squawks, and reached a clearing. The parrot was sitting on a rock. And it looked just like a giant hand with big finger pointing off to a cave.

"Sorry!" squawked the parrot.

"Don't apologise!" said Angelo. "Well done!"

Angelo and Dandy ran to the cave. There was a notice outside. 'Here be Black Jack's treasure!'

"Anyone could find this!" said Angelo.

"Only if they had a map," said Dandy. "Black Jack was our uncle! He gave me that old book. Nobody else has seen it!"

The cave was dark inside, but being a cat, Angelo could see

fairly well. He found a box and dragged it out to Dandy.

"Treasure?" asked Dandy.

"It's a small box," said Angelo.

"Black Jack wasn't a very successful pirate," said Dandy.

They opened the box, and there tucked in the corner was a small bag and a note.

'Sorry nephews,' read the note, 'this is all the treasure I have, but as you have followed the map, it's all yours. Your uncle Black Jack.'

"There's enough for your brother to retire on," said Angelo with a laugh.

"And enough to repaint the Yankee Doodle," said Dandy.

"Sorry!" squawked Sorry.

"Oh, and for a few sunflower seeds!" said Angelo.

"My Best Friend's A Tottamus!"

Grandpa was collecting Bod and Posie from their school and decided to take them to the swings on the green before going home.

Bod and Posie sat on the swing seats while Grandpa pushed them higher and higher.

"Enough, Grandpa!" Bod called out suddenly. "I'm going to the slide, now!"

Bod ran off to the slide, and climbed the ladder and slid down a few times.

On his fourth climb, he noticed something at the bottom of the slide. He slid down.

"Hello," he said. The something was a someone.

"Hello," replied the someone.

"Who are you?" asked Bod,

looking down at his new friend.

"I'm Sam," said the newcomer. "We've just moved into the house by the end of the green."

"We're up the other end," said Bod, squatting down to talk. "I'm Bod. That's my big sister Posie, on the swing, and that's my Grandpa pushing her. I've also got a baby sister, Em, but she doesn't really count, because she can't play properly yet."

"Are you at school?" asked Sam. "I start on Monday."

"Great! You might be in my class." said Bod. "Do you want to play?"

"I find it a bit difficult to sit on the swings," said Sam. "But I'll try to climb the slide."

Sam clambered up the slide, and slid down on his tummy.

Bod and Sam played for a while together until Grandpa called for Bod to go home.

Bod ran home and through the gate and into the kitchen.

"I've just met the new people at the end of the green," he told his mother. "At least, I met Sam. He's going to school on Monday. He can't go on swings very well, but he can slide all right. And he does it on his tummy. He might be in my class. Can he come to tea? He's a tottamus.

"Slow down Bod," said his mother.

"Can he come to tea?" asked Bod again.

"Is this Bod's new friend?" asked Grandpa, as he walked into the kitchen.

"He's a tottamus, isn't he, Grandpa," said Bod.

"Yes," laughed Grandpa. "I suppose he is!"

"I can't wait," said Bod's mother.

The weekend passed, and on Monday Bod was very excited and ate his breakfast extra fast and dressed himself, which was most unusual. The buttons were slightly out and his shoes were on the wrong feet, but apart from that he didn't do too badly!

"Can he come for tea?" Bod asked again.

"Tomorrow, if his mother says it's all right," said Bod's mother.

"Grandpa will ask her this morning, as he says he knows who to ask."

Bod skipped out the door, singing. "My best friend's a tottamus!"

Grandpa laughed again, and Bod's mother looked very puzzled.

"A tottamus?" she whispered to Grandpa.

"All will become clear," he smiled, tapping the side of his nose.

Sam was in Bod's class, and Bod immediately sat by him at the table.

"We can be best friends,"

Bod whispered to Sam.

"Yes, please," Sam whispered back.

That evening Bod burst through the door, again singing, "Sam is in my class! My best friend's a tottamus! He can come to tea!"

Bod's mother had to wait another day to meet Bod's new and best friend. She made some jelly as she knew it was Bod's favourite, and a cake.

"I hope Sam likes cake," she said to Baby Em who was in her high chair.

School finished and the bears' mother waited for Bod and Posie to come home.

She heard them running down the path and the door opened. Grandpa walked in, followed by Posie and Bod.

"Here he is," said Bod.

"Here's my friend, Sam."

Sam came into the kitchen, smiling shyly at Bod's mother.

"Hello," he said.

"Aah," said Bod's mother, with a smile. "I was wandering who to expect. Bod has been saying all weekend that his best friend is a tottamus! He's had me a little puzzled."

"Well, he is a tottamus!" said Bod.

"I don't mind," said Sam. "I like that name."

"Then it's teatime, and cake and jelly all round!" said the bears' mother. Bod's new friend sat down.

"Tot-tot-tot-mus!" declared Baby Em, and she reached out to stoke Sam's back. "Tot-tot-tot-mus!"

Sam grinned and disappeared shyly into his shell, and then played 'beep-bo!' with Baby Em, who screamed with delight.

A Day At The Races

Bod was at the barber shop with Father Bear, having his fur trimmed. It had just been washed and he was looking around the shop. The ladies' side was full - ladies were having their hair curled and their nails polished.

"Why are there so many people here?" Bod said in surprise.

"It's race day on Saturday, Bod," said the barber, trimming away. "Everyone wants to look their best."

"Are we going?" Bod asked his father.

Father Bear nodded.

Bod looked at the pictures in a magazine while his father was having his own trim.

'A Day at the Races' read the headline on one page.

"Is this about the same kind of racing?" he asked his father.

Father Bear nodded.

"That's the smart way to go racing," he said.

Bod looked at the pictures. There were lots of people dressed up - the men in tall, shiny top hats and long-tailed coats, and the ladies were wearing beautiful dresses and big hats.

"Posie and I can dress up like that!" declared Bod.

The Barber had finished, so Bod and his father left the shop.

"Will we see you at the races Bod?" asked the barber.

"You certainly shall," said Bod.

Bod and his father wandered down the street, looking in the shops. They came to the tailor's shop and there, in the window, was a dummy wearing a tall, shiny top hat and a long-tailed coat.

"That's what I want to wear," sighed Bod, looking at the dummy.

They went round the corner towards home, and walked past the back of the shop.

"Ooh look!" squealed Bod, as he spotted something about to be thrown away.

"Look!" he squealed again, as he looked closer. It was an old dummy, with a very old coat on it, it was a long-tailed coat.

"Ooh look!" squealed Bod for a third time. Some men were about to throw the dummy on the rubbish tip.

"Oh no!" cried Bod. "Please don't throw that coat away!"

The men stopped.

"Hello Bod," they said. "Rosie's not with you? How's Baby Em?"

"She's not with me. I've just had my hair cut," said Bod in a hurry. "Please don't throw that coat away."

"What - this old thing?" said

one of the men. "We were just about to."

"Could I possibly have it?" asked Bod.

"We could try it on you," said the men.

There was an old cracked mirror in the yard and Bod stood in front of it in the enormous coat. One of the men held most of the coat behind Bod and peered over his shoulder.

"It suits you, Bod," he said. "Now all you need is a hat."

"A hat!" cried Bod. "Where am I going to find a hat?"

Bod and his father set off across the green towards home.

"I've just had an idea," said Bod's father. "We'll just go to see your Nana and Grandpa."

It was a short walk and Bod and his father were soon walking up the front path to his grandparents' home.

"Grandpa!" cried Bod, when his grandfather opened the door. "This is unexpected!" declared Grandpa.

"You have something in your garden that Bod may find useful!" said Father Bear.

"Oh yes?" asked Grandpa. He led the way through the house.

"What do you see?" asked Bod's father, as they stood at the kitchen door.

"Nothing!" declared Bod, looking about.

"Have another look. What do you need?" said his father.

Grandpa looked at Bod and shrugged his shoulders. He

certainly had no idea! Bod
looked again, and suddenly
shouted out. He ran off to
Grandpa's vegetable patch. He
jumped up at the scarecrow
guarding the patch and knocked
off its hat. He then grabbed it
and ran back to his father.

"Can I borrow this?" he
asked, holding a rather sorry
looking, battered top hat. "It's
just what I need for Saturday!

"I'll clean it up for him," said
Father Bear. "It's for Saturday's
race day.

"Posie can wear the dress that
Nana made," said Bod.

At home, Bod tried on the
coat. He stood in front of the
mirror.

"A few changes and it will be
perfect," said Bod's mother. She
also found a large hat for Posie
to wear.

Father Bear mended and cleaned the tall top hat until it was shiny.

The day of the races dawned. Bod and Posie jumped out of bed and raced to eat their breakfast.

"Today's the day," they said to their parents at the breakfast table.

Mother Bear and Father Bear helped Bod and Posie to get ready in all their finery, and then the whole family, with Baby Em, left for the race course.

Bod and Posie walked proudly ahead of the family.

"What handsome bears!" they heard someone say.

"Don't they look smart!" Father Bear heard somebody else say. He was very proud of Bod and Posie, too.

At the race course, the Bear family headed for the track to watch the first race. Bod and Posie stood near the finishing line.

As they watched the first race, someone came to talk to their father.

"I'm sure they would love to," they heard their father say. He then called them over and whispered in their ears.

"Ooh, yes!" they cried, and they all followed the man to the circle where the horses were taken after the race.

Bod and Posie followed to the winner's stand, and there they waited while the first race finished.

The winning horse and jockey were led in. The proud owner walked beside them. "We present you with the gold cup, and a rosette!" said Bod and Posie, as they gave the prizes for the first race.

"Well done, Bod and Posie!" said Father and Mother Bear.

"Three cheers for Bod and Posie, the best-dressed teddies of the day!" called the crowd. "Hip hip hooray!"

The Picnic

The day of the village picnic dawned and the animals were off to the 'big house'. There were beautiful gardens and meadows and there was the maze.

Mrs Badger had spent the previous day baking and Mayor

Badger piled the cakes, buns and pastries into his handcart.

Fox and Mrs Fox met the Badgers and all the other animals at the bridge by the green. They carried picnic baskets and hampers between them and Badger pushed his handcart.

"We're off," said Badger, and off they went.

"We can try the maze after lunch," said Mouse. "We could even have a prize for whoever gets to the middle first."

"One of Mrs Badger's fruit buns, I think," suggested Fox.

"Good idea," said Owl. "Can I eat it with one wing bandaged?" He had fallen and hurt his wing.

"You've got to get there first," laughed Fox.

The walk was happy and everyone was ready to eat their lunch when they arrived at the green near the maze.

"Look, there's a peacock!" cried Jack.

"No, it's not," said Mouse. "It's one of the hedges cut into the shape of a peacock. Look, there are more animals and birds."

The animals looked to see bushes cut into all sorts of creatures.

"That's where the maze starts," said Badger.

The animals settled down to their lunch right by the maze

entrance.

"Make sure we leave enough for our tea," suggested Mrs Badger, as she saw how quickly her delicious baking was disappearing.

Jack couldn't wait any longer. He jumped up, sweeping crumbs from his lap, saying, "Come on, let's go into the maze!"

Other animals licked their lips and fingers and stood. Mrs Fox and Mrs Badger started to sort things out.

"Come on," said Fox. "Let's go."

"We'll stay here, and get tea ready," said Mrs Fox. "I'm sure you'll need something to eat when you find your way out."

"That's a good idea,"

decided Fox. "We shouldn't be too long. It should be easy enough to get to the middle."

"We'll just see how long it takes you to get out!" declared Mrs Fox.

The animals disappeared behind the bush wall, between two peacocks.

"Turn right here!" called Jack.

"Left at this corner," said Fox.

"Oops! Dead end," came Owl's voice.

"Turn around," said Badger.

Mrs Fox and Mrs Badger smiled as they heard the voices fade into the distance as the animals went further into the maze.

"Oh well," said Mrs Badger. "A quick tidy and we can have a stroll."

Within a few minutes the picnic site was tidy and Mrs Fox and Mrs Badger wandered off through the gardens.

Fox was right and it didn't take long for the animals to get to the middle of the maze.

Jack dashed to the square in the centre.

"A peacock again!" he cried, as he reached the cut bush. "They like peacocks here, don't they!"

"It seems they do, young Jack," agreed Owl.

"Jack's won the special cake," said Mole. "Now, which way is out?"

"I don't know," said Mouse. "We changed direction so many times, I don't know which way we're facing now."

"Turn left, then right," said Fox.

"No, straight on," said Owl.

"I'm sure it's right, then left," said Jack.

"I think we should

all stay together," said Badger. "Wherever we go, we don't want to lose anyone."

"Owl, you can fly out!" cried Jack.

"Not for a few days," said Owl, holding up his bandaged wing.

"It seems we have a slight problem," said Fox, "and I'm looking forward to my tea!"

"I could dig my way out," suggested Mole.

"Can you dig a hole big enough for me?" asked Owl.

"Aah," said Mole, thinking

again.

"Squirrel's not here, is he?" said Badger, looking around the group.

"No, visiting family," said Fox.

"We need height," said Owl, "to look over the top."

"Peacocks!" declared Jack.

"Pardon, young Jack," said Badger.

"Peacocks," repeated Jack. "The peacock in the middle is pointing the way!"

"What do you mean?" asked Fox.

"There are a lot of bushy animals all over the maze," said Jack, "but the only peacocks are at the entrance and in the centre!"

"He's right!" said Fox. "Well spotted!"

"Up on my back, Jack," said Badger. "Let's see where those two peacocks are."

Jack scrambled onto Badger's shoulders and looked around.

"There!" he suddenly shouted, pointing.

"That's it then, out we go," said Badger. "Stay close everybody."

The animals followed Jack's direction, as he lead them

towards the two peacocks at the entrance to the maze.

Ten minutes later the animals emerged from the maze.

"Oh!" said Mrs Fox. She and Mrs Badger were just returning from their walk. "We didn't expect to see you so soon!"

"Aah well, my dear," said Fox. "Frankly, neither did we!"

"We can thank Jack and the peacocks," said Badger.

"And who won the prize cake?" asked Mrs Badger.

"Jack!" declared all the animals.

Jack stood and smiled as he bit into his prize cake. From somewhere in the gardens, a real peacock screeched.